For Anna and Katy

The Birthday Presents
Text copyright © 1999 by Paul Stewart. Illustrations copyright © 1999 by Chris Riddell.
First published in Great Britain in 1999 by Andersen Press Ltd. First American edition, 2000
Printed in Italy. All rights reserved. ISBN 0-06-028279-7
Library of Congress catalog card number: 99-63084
http://www.harperchildrens.com

The Birthday Presents

by Paul Stewart

pictures by Chris Riddell

HarperCollins Publishers

"Hedgehog," said Rabbit. "When is your birthday?"
"I don't know," said Hedgehog.
"Neither do I." Rabbit sighed.

"If I don't know when my birthday is,"
said Hedgehog, "how could you?"
"I mean," said Rabbit, "I don't know
when *my* birthday is."
"Oh," said Hedgehog.

As the sun sank behind the trees,
Hedgehog and Rabbit thought sadly about
all the birthdays they would never have.

"I have an idea," said Hedgehog.
"Let's celebrate our birthdays tomorrow."
"They might not be tomorrow," said Rabbit.
"But they *might* be," said Hedgehog.
"It would be a shame to miss them if they are."

"You're right," said Rabbit. "That's a good idea.
We will wish each other happy birthday."
"And give each other presents," said Hedgehog.
"Presents?" yawned Rabbit.
"Birthday presents," said Hedgehog. "That's what
birthdays are *for*."

Later, as Hedgehog snuffled for slugs
beneath the plump, silver moon,
he wondered what sort of present
he should give his friend.

Hedgehog thought about the burrow
where Rabbit was fast asleep.
"How silent, gloomy, and damp it must be.
How dark!"

An empty bottle glinted down by the lake.
Hedgehog looked at the bottle.
He looked at the moonlight on the water.
"That's it!" he cried.

Hedgehog filled the bottle with the bright water.

"A bottle of moonlight will be my present," he said. Then he wrapped it up and went to bed.

Rabbit woke up early, too excited to stay asleep.
"What present should I give Hedgehog?"
he wondered.

Rabbit thought of his friend,
sleeping out in the wide open.
"How frightening and noisy it must be.
How bright!"

In the corner of his burrow,
he spied his useful tin.
"The very thing!" he cried.

Rabbit filled the tin with warm,
snuggly darkness and patted
it down with his paw.
"A box of coziness," he said.

He pressed the lid into place

and wrapped it all up with straw.
"Hedgehog will love my present."

Evening came, and the two friends met.
"Rabbit," said Hedgehog. "Happy birthday!"
"Happy birthday to *you*, Hedgehog!" said Rabbit.

"Here is your present," said Hedgehog.
Rabbit tore off the leaf wrapping.
"It's a bottle of moonlight," said Hedgehog,
"so that you will no longer be afraid
of your very, very dark burrow."

"But I'm not—"
Rabbit stopped.
"Thank you," he said. "It's a wonderful present."

"And here is *your* present," said Rabbit.
Hedgehog tore off the straw wrapping.

"It's a box of coziness," said Rabbit,
"so that you will no longer be
disturbed by the bright, noisy day."

"But I'm not—"
Hedgehog stopped.
"It's just what I've always wanted," he said.

In the middle of the dark night,
Rabbit woke up and looked at his present.
"Dear Hedgehog," he said.
"A bottle of moonlight, indeed."
He took out the stopper
and drank the water inside.
"I can fill it with water every day," said Rabbit.
"Then I will never be thirsty in the night again."

At the end of the long, rustling night,
Hedgehog noticed his present.
"Dear Rabbit," he said sleepily.
"A box of coziness, indeed."
Hedghog opened the lid and looked inside.
"It's a slug-catcher!" he said.
"I will never be hungry if I wake up in the
middle of the day again."

That evening, Hedgehog found Rabbit
down by the lake.
"Do you like your bottle of light?" he asked.

"Yes," said Rabbit. "It's the best present
I've ever gotten. Do you like your box of coziness?"
"Yes," said Hedgehog. "It's the best present
I've ever gotten."

Together, the two friends watched the sun
turn from orange to red.

"Hedgehog," said Rabbit, rubbing his eyes.
"When will we have another birthday?"
"Soon," said Hedgehog. "Very soon."